Anonymous

The History of Sindbad the Sailor

Containing an Account of his Several Surprising Voyages

Anonymous

The History of Sindbad the Sailor
Containing an Account of his Several Surprising Voyages

ISBN/EAN: 9783744750202

Printed in Europe, USA, Canada, Australia, Japan

Cover: Foto ©Andreas Hilbeck / pixelio.de

More available books at **www.hansebooks.com**

THE
HISTORY
OF
SINDBAD
THE
SAILOR :

CONTAINING

AN ACCOUNT

OF HIS SEVERAL

SURPRISING VOYAGES

AND

MIRACULOUS ESCAPES.

EMBELLISHED WITH ELEGANT CUTS.

GAINSBROUGH :

Printed at Mozley and Co's Lilliputian Book-Manufactory,

PRICE SIXPENCE.

1796.

THE
HISTORY
OF
SINDBAD
THE
SAILOR.

His First Voyage.

MY father left me a confiderable eftate, moft part of which I fpent
during my youth ; but I perceived my er-
ror, and called to mind that riches were pe-
rifhable, and quickly confumed by fuch ill huf-
bands as myfelf. I farther confidered, that, by
my irregular way of living, I wretchedly mif-
fpent my time, which is the moft valuable thing

A 3

in the world. I remembered the saying of the great Solomon, which I had frequently heard from my father, that *Death is more tolerable than Poverty*. Being struck with those reflections, I gathered together the ruins of my estate, and sold all my moveables in the public market to the highest bidder. Then I entered into a contract with some merchants, that traded by sea ; I took the advice of such as I thought most capable to give it me ; and, resolving to improve what money I had, I went to Balsora, a port on the Persian Gulph, and embarked with several merchants, who joined with me to fit out a ship on purpose.

We set sail, and steered our course towards the East-Indies, through the Persian Gulph. At first I was troubled with the sea-sickness, but speedily recovered my health, and was not afterwards troubled with that disease.

In our voyage we touched at several islands, where we sold or exchanged our goods. One day, whilft under fail, we were becalmed near a little ifland, even almoft within the furface of the water, which refembled a green meadow. The captain ordered his fails to be furled, and fuffered fuch perfons, as had a mind, to land up-on the ifland, amongft whom I was one.

But, while we were diverting ourfelves with eating and drinking, and refrefhing ourfelves from the fatigue of the fea, the ifland trembled all of a fudden, and fhook us terribly.

They perceived the trembling of the ifland on board the fhip, and called to us to reimbark fpeedily, or we fhould all be loft; for what we took for an ifland, was only the back of a whale. The nimbleft got into the floop, others betook themfelves to fwim; but, for my part, I was ftill upon the back of the whale when he dived into the fea, and had time only to catch hold of a piece of wood that we had brought out of the fhip to make a fire. Mean while the cap-tain, having received thofe on board, who were in the floop, and taken up fome of thofe that ſwam, reſolved to improve the favourable gale that was juſt riſen, and hoiſting his ſails, purſued his voyage, ſo that it was impoſſible to recover the ſhip.

Thus I was expoſed to the mercy of the waves, and ſtruggled for my life all the reſt of of the day and the following night. Next morning I found my ſtrength gone, and deſpaired of ſaving my life, when a wave threw me happily againſt an iſland. The bank was high and rugged, ſo that I ſhould ſcarcely have got up, had it not been for ſome roots of trees, which fortune ſeemed to have preſerved in this place for my ſafety. Being got up, I lay down upon the ground half dead, until ſuch time as the ſun appeared. Then, though I was very feeble, both by reaſon of my hard labour and want of victuals, I creeped along to ſeek for ſome herbs fit to eat, and had not only the good luck to find ſome, but likewiſe a ſpring of excellent water, which contributed much to recover me. After this I advanced father into the Iſland, & came at laft into a fine plain, where I perceived a horfe feeding at a great diftance. I went towards him betwixt hopes and fear, not knowing whether I was going to lofe my life, or to fave it. When I came near it, I perceived it to be a very fine horfe, tied to a ftake. Whilft I looked upon him, I heard the voice of a man from under ground, who immediately appeared to me, and afked who I was. I gave him an account of my adventure, after which, taking me by the hand, he led me into a cave, where there were feveral other people, no lefs amazed to fee me, than I was to fee them.

I ate fome victuals which they offered me, and then, having afked them what they did in fuch a defert place ? they anfwered, that they were grooms belonging to King Mihrage, fovereign of the ifland ; and that every year, at the fame feafon, they brought thither the king's horfes, and faftened them as I faw that horfe, till they were wafhed with the water of a neighbouring pool ; by virtue of which extraordinary water, they were rendered ftronger and more beautiful. They added, that they were to go home to-morrow, and had I been one day later, I muft have perifhed, becaufe the inhabited part of the ifland was at a greater diftance, and it would have been impoffible for me to have got thither without a guide.

Next morning they returned with their horfes to the capital of the ifland, took me with them, and prefented me to King Mihrage. He afked me who I was, By what adventure I came into his dominions? And, after I had fatified him, he told me he was much concerned for my misfortune, and at the fame time ordered that I fhould want nothing, which his officers were fo generous and careful as to fee exactly fulfilled. .

Being a merchant, I frequented men of my own profeffion, and particularly enquired for thofe who were ftrangers, if perhaps I might hear any news from Bagdad, or find an opportunity to return thither. For King Mihrage's capital is fituated on the bank of the fea, and

has a fine harbour where ships arrive daily from
the different quarters of the world.   I frequented also the society of the learned Indians, and
took delight to hear them discourse; but withal,
I took care to make my court regularly to the
king, and conversed with the governors to the
petty kings, his tributaries, that were about
him. They asked me a thousand questions about
my country; and I being willing to inform myself as to their laws and customs, asked them
every thing which I thought worth knowing.

As I was one day at the port after my return
a ship arrived, and as soon as she cast anchor
they began to unload her, and the merchants on
board ordered their goods to be carried into the
magazine. As I cast my eye upon some bales,
and looked to the name, I found my own, and
perceived the bales to be the same that I had
embarked at Balsora.   I also knew the captain :
but being persuaded that he believed me to be
drowned, I went and asked him whose bales
these were ?   He replied, that they belonged to

a merchant of Bagdad called Sindbad, who came to fea with him ; but one day, being near an ifland, as we thought, he went afhore with feveral other paffengers upon this fuppcfed ifland which was only a monftrous whale, that lay afleep upon the furface of the water : but as foon as he felt the heat of the fire, they had kindled on his back to drefs fome victuals, he began to move, and dived under water ; moft of the perfons who were upon him perifhed, and among them unfortunate Sindbad. Thofe bales belonged to him, and I am refolved to trade with them, until I meet with fome of his family, to whom I may return the profit. Captain, fays I, I am that Sindbad whom you thought to be dead, and thofe bales are mine. When the captain heard me fpeak thus : " O " heaven, fays he, who can we ever truft now a " days, there is no faith left among men. I faw " Sindbad perifh with my own eyes, and the " paffengers on board faw it as well as I, & yet " you tell me that you are Sindbad ; what in-

" pudence is this ? To look on you, one would
" take you to be a man of probity, and yet you
" tell a horrible falſhood, in order to poſſeſs
" yourſelf of what does not belong to you."—
" Have patience, captain, replied I, do me the
" favour to hear what I have to ſay."—" Very
" well, ſays he, ſpeak, I am ready to hear
" you." Then I told him how I eſcaped, and
by what adventure I met with the grooms of
King Mihrage, who brought me to his court.

He began to abate of his confidence upon my
diſcourſe, and was ſoon perſuaded that I was no
cheat : for there came people from his ſhip, who
knew me, made me great compliments, and
teſtified a great deal of joy to ſee me alive. At
laſt he knew me himſelf, and embracing me,
" Heaven be praiſed, ſays he, for your happy
" eſcape, I cannot enough expreſs my joy for
" it : there are your goods, take and do with
" them what you will." I thanked him acknowledged hi probity, and in requital, offered

him part of my goods as a prefent, which he generoufly refufed.

I took out what was moft valuable in my bales and prefented it to King Mihrage, who, knowing my misfortune, afked me how I came by fuch rarities ? I acquainted him with the whole ftory : he was mightly pleafed at my good luck, accepted my prefent, and gave me one much more confiderable in return. Upon this I took leave of him, and went on board the fame fhip, after I had exchanged my goods with the commodities of that country. I carried with me wood of aloes, fanders, camphire, nutmegs, cloves, pepper, and ginger. We paffed by feveral iflands, and at laft arrived at Balfora, from whence I came to Bagdad, with the value of 100,000 fequins. My family and I received one another with all the tranfports that can happen from true and fincere friendfhip. I bought flaves of both fexes, fine lands, and built me a great houfe. And thus I fettled myfelf, refolving to forget the miferies I had fuffered, and to enjoy the pleafures of life.

SINDBAD

THE
SECOND VOYAGE
OF
SINBAD
THE
SAILOR.

I Defigned, after my firft voyage, to fpend the reft of my days at Bagdad ; but it was not long ere I grew weary of an idle life. My inclination to trade revived. I bought goods proper for the commerce I defigned, and put to fea a fecond time with merchants of known probity. We embarked on board a good fhip. and, after recommending ourfelves to God, fet fail : we traded from ifland to ifland, and exchanged com-

B

modities with great profit.   One day we landed
in an ifle covered with feveral forts of fruit-trees,
but fo defert, that we could neither fee man nor
horfe upon it.   We went to take a little frefh
air in the meadows, and along the ftreams that
watered them.   Whilft fome diverted themfelves
with gathering flowers, and others with gathering fruits, I took my wine and provifions, and
fat down by a ftream betwixt two great trees,
which formed a curious fhade.   I made a very
good meal, and afterwards fell afleep.   I cannot tell how long I flept ; but when I waked
the fhip was gone.

I was very much furprized to find the fhip
gone ; I got up, looked about every where, and
could not fee one of the merchants who landed
with me.   At laft I perceived the fhip under
fail ; but at fuch a diftance, that I loft fight of
her in a very little time.

I leave you to guefs at my melancholy reflections in this fad condition : I was like to die of
grief ; I cried out fadly ; I beat my head and

breaſt, and threw myſelf down upon the ground, where ! lay a long time in a terrible agony, one afflicting thought ſucceeding another more afflicting.   I upbraided myſelf an hundred times, for not being content with the product of my firſt voyage, that might very well have ſerved me all my life. But all this was in vain, and my repentance out of ſeaſon.

At laſt I reſigned myſelf to the will of God; and not knowing what to do, I climbed up to the top of a great tree, from whence I looked about on all ſides, to ſee if there were any thing that could give me hopes.   When I looked towards the ſea, I could ſee nothing but ſky and water; but, looking towards the land, I ſaw ſomething white; and coming down from the tree, I took up what proviſions I had left, and went towards, it, the diſtance being ſo great, that I could not diſtinguiſh what it was.

When I came nearer, I thought it to be a white bowl, of a prodigious height and bigneſs; and when I came up to it, I touched it, and found it to be very smooth. I went round to see if it was open on any side, but saw it was not, and that there was no climbing up to the top of it, it was so smooth. It was at least 50 paces round.

By this time the sun was ready to set, and all of a sudden the sky became as dark as if it had been covered with a thick cloud. I was much astonished at this sudden darkness, but much more when I found it was occasioned by a bird of a monstrous size, that came flying towards me. I remembered a fowl called Roc, that I had often heard mariners speak of, and conceived that the great bowl, which I so much admired, must needs be its egg. In short, the bird lighted and sat over the egg to hatch it. As I perceived her coming I crept close to the egg, so that I had before me one of the legs of the bird, that was as big as the trunk of a tree ; I tied myself strongly to it with the cloth that went round my turban, in hopes that when the roc flew away the next morning, she would carry me with her

out of this defart ifland.   And after having, paffed the night in this condition the bird actually
flew away next morning, as foon as it was day,
and carried me fo high that I could not fee the
earth ; fhe afterwards defcended all of a fudden
with fo much rapidity, that I loft my fenfes.
But when the roc was fat, and that I found
myfelf on the ground, I fpeedily untied the knot,
and had fcarce done, when the bird, having taken up a ferpent of a monftrous length in her
bill, flew ftrait away.

The place where it left me was a very deep
valley, encompaffed on all fides with mountains
fo high, that they feemed to reach above the
clouds, and fo full of fteep rocks, that there was
no poffibility to get out of the valley.   This was
a new perplexity upon me ; fo that when I
compared this place with the defart ifland the
roc brought me from, I found that I gained nothing by the change.

As I walked through this valley, I perceived
it was ftrewed with diamonds, fome of which

were of a furprifing bignefs. I took a great
deal of pleafure to look upon them ; but fpeedily
faw at a diftance fuch objects as very much di-
minifhed my fatisfaction, and which I could not
look upon without terror ; that was a great number of ferpents, fo big, and fo long, that the
leaft of them was capable of fwallowing an elephant. They retired in the day-time to their
dens, where they hid themfelves from the roc,
their enemy, and did not come out but in the
night-time.

I fpent the day in walking about the valley,
refting myfelf at times in fuch palaces as I thought
moft commodious. When night came on, I
went into a cave, where I thought I might be in
fafety ; I ftopped the mouth of it, which was
low and ftrait, with a great ftone to preferve me
from the ferpents ; but not fo exactly fitted as to
hinder light from coming in. I fupped on part
of my provifions ; but the ferpents, which began
to appear, hiffing about in the mean time, put
me into fuch extreme fear, that you may eafily

imagine I did not fleep. When day appeared, the ferpents retired, and I came out of the cave trembling ; I can juftly fay, that I walked a long time upon diamonds, without having a mind to touch any of them. At laft I fat down, and notwithftanding my uneafinefs, and not having fhut my eyes during the night, I fell afleep, after having eat a little more of my provifions. But I had fcarce fhut my eyes, when fomething, that fell by me with a great noife, awaked me, and that was a great piece of frefh meat ; and at the fame time I faw feveral others fall down from the rocks in different places.

I always looked upon it to be a fable, when I heard mariners and others difcourfe of the valley of diamonds, and of the ftratagem made ufe of by fome merchants to get jewels from thence, but then I found it to be true. For, in reality, thofe merchants come to the neighbourhood of this valley, when the eagles have young ones, and throwing great joints of meat into this valley, the diamonds, upon whofe points they fall,

ſtick to them ; the eagles, which are ſtronger in
this country than any where elſe, fall down with
great force upon thoſe pieces of meat, and carry
them to their neſts upon the top of the rocks, to
feed their young eagles with ; at which time the
merchants, running to their neſts, frighten the
eagles by their noiſe, and take away the diamonds which ſtick to the meat. And this ſtra-
tagem they make uſe of to get the diamonds out
of the valley, which is ſurrounded with ſuch
precipices that nobody can enter it.

I believed ever till then, that it was not poſſible for me to get out of this abyſs, which I
looked upon as my grave ; but then I changed
my mind ; for the falling in of thoſe pieces of
meat, put me in hopes of a way of ſaving my
life.

I began to gather together the greateſt diamonds that I could ſee, and put them into the
leather bag where I uſed to carry my proviſions.
I afterwards took the largeſt piece of meat I
could find, tied it cloſe round me with the cloth

of my turban, and then laid myself upon the
ground, with my face downward, the bag of diamonds being tied fast to my girdle, that it could
not possibly drop off.

I had scarce laid me down, till the eagles
came, each of them seized a piece of meat, and
one of the strongest having taken me up, with
the piece of meat on my back, carried me to his
nest on the top of the mountain. The merchants fell straightway a shouting to frighten the
eagles ; and when they had obliged them to quit
their prey, one of them came up to the nest
where I was : he was very much afraid when he
saw me ; but recovering himself, instead of en-
quiring how I came thither, he began to quarrel
with me, and asked why I stole his goods.
" You will treat me, replied I, with more civi-
" lity, when you know me better. Don't trou-
" ble yourself, I have diamonds enough for you
" and me too, more than all the other merchants
" together. If they have any, it is by chance ;
" but I chose for myself, in the bottom of the
C

" valley, all thofe which you fee in this bag ;"
and having fpoke thofe words, I fhewed them
to him. I had fcarce done fpeaking, when the
other merchants came trooping about us, very
much aftonifhed to fee me, but they were much
more furprized when I told them my ftory ; yet
they did not fo much admire my ftratagem to
fave myfelf, as my courage to attempt it.

They carried me to the place where they ftaid
all together, and there having opened my bag,
they were furprifed at the largenefs of my diamonds, and confeffed, that in all the courts
where they had been, they never faw any, that
came near them. I prayed the merchant to
whom the neft belonged whither I was carried,
for every merchant had his own, to take as many for his fhare as he pleafed : he contented himfelf with one, and that too the leaft of them ;
and when I preffed him to take more, without
fear of doing me any injury, " No fays he, I
" am very well fatisfied with this, which is va-

" luable enough to fave me the trouble of mak-
" ing any more voyages, to raife as great a for-
" tune as I defire "

I fpent the night with thofe merchants, to
whom I told my ftory a fecond time, for the fatisfaction of thofe who had not heard it.   I could
not moderate my joy, when I found myfelf delivered from the danger I have mentioned ; I
thought myfelf to be in a dream, and could
fcarce believe myfelf to be out of hazard.

The merchants had thrown their pieces of
meat into the valley for feveral days.   And each
of them been fatisfied with the diamonds that
had fallen to his lot, we left the place next
morning all together, and travelled near high
mountains, where there were ferpents of a prodigious length, which we had the good fortune
to efcape.   We took the firft port we came at,
and came to the ifle of Roha, where the trees
grow that yield camphire.   This tree is fo large
and its branches fo thick, that 100 men may eafily fit under its fhade.   The juice of which the

camphire is made, runs out from a hole bored in
the upper part of the tree, is received in a yaffel,
where it grows to a confiftency, and becomes
what we call camphire ; and the Juice thus drawn
out, the tree withers and dies.

There is in this ifland the rhinoceros, a creature lefs than the elephant, but greater than a
buffalo ; they have a horn upon their nofe, about
a cubit long ; this horn is folid, and cleft in the
middle from one end to the other, and there is
upon it white draughts, reprefenting the figure
of a man.   The rhinoceros fights with the elephant, runs his horn into his belly, and carries
him off upon his head : but the blood and the fat
of the elephant running into his eyes, and making him blind, he falls to the ground ; and that
which is aftonifhing, the roc comes and carries
them both away in her claws, to be meat for her
young ones.

I pafs over many other things peculiar to this
ifland, left I fhould be troublefome to you.
Here I exchanged fome of my diamonds for

good merchandife. From thence we went to other ides, and at laft, having touched at feveral trading towns of the firm land, we landed at Balfora'; from whence I went to Bagdad. There I immediately gave great alms to the poor, and lived honourably upon the vaft riches I had brought, and gained with fo much fatigue.

SINDBAD

THE
THIRD VOYAGE
OF
SINDBAD
THE
SAILOR.

THE pleasures of the life which I then led, soon made me forget the risques I had run in my two former voyages; but being then in the flower of my age, I grew weary of living without business, and hardening myself against the thought of any danger I might incur, I went from Bagdad with the richest commodities of the country of Balsora. There I embarked again with other merchants. We made a long navigation, and touched at feveral ports, with which we drove a confiderable commerce. One day being out in the main ocean, we were attacked by a horrible tempeft, which made us lofe our courfe.

The tempeft continued feveral days, and brought us before the port of an ifland, where the captain was very unwilling to enter, but we were obliged to caft anchor there. When we had furled our fails, the captain told us, that this, and fome other neighbouring iflands, were inhabited by hairy favages who would fpeedily attack us ; and, though they were but dwarfs, yet our misfortune was fuch, that we muft make no refiftance, for they were more in number than the locufts ; and if we happened to kill one of them, they would all fall upon us and deftroy us.

This difcourfe of the captain put the whole equipage into a great confternation, and we found very foon to our coft, that what he told us was but too true. An innumerable multitiude of frightful favages, covered all over with red hair and about two foot high, came fwimming to-

wards us, and encompaffed our ship in a little
time. They fpoke to us as they came near, but
we underftood not their language ; they climbed
up the fides of the fhip with fo much agility as
furprized us.   We beheld all this with a mortal
fear, without daring to offer at defending ourfelves, or to fpeak one word to divert them from
their mifchievous defign. In fhort, they took
down our fails, cut the cable, and hauling to the
fhóre, made us all get out, and afterwards carried the fhip into another ifland, from whence
they came.   All travellers carefully avoided that
ifland, where they left, us, it being very dangerous to ftay there, for a reafon you fhall hear
anon, but we were forced to bear our affliction
with patience.

   We went forward into the ifland, where we
found fome fruits and herbs to prolong our lives
as long as we could ; but we expected nothing
but death. As we went on, we perceived at a
diftance a great pile of building, and made towards it.   We found it to be a palace well built

& very high, with a gate of ebony of two leaves which we thruſt open. On entering the court, we ſaw before us a vaſt apartment, with a porch, having on one ſide a heap of men's bones, and on the other, a vaſt number of roaſting ſpits. We trembled at this ſpeÉtacle, and being weary with travelling, our legs failed under us, we fell to the ground, being ſeized with a mortal fear, and lay along time immoveable.

The ſun was ſet, and whilſt we were in this lamentable condition juſt now mentioned, the gate of the apartment opened with a great noiſe, and there came out the horrible figure of a black man, as high as a tall palm-tree. He had but one eye, and that in the middle of his forehead, where it looked as red as a burning coal. His fore-teeth were very long and ſharp, and came without his mouth, which was as deep as that of a horſe. His upper lip hung down upon his breaſt, his ears reſembled thoſe of an elephant, and covered his ſhoulders ; and his nails were as long and crooked as the talons of the greateſt birds. At the fight of fo frightful a giant, we loft all fenfe, and lay men dead.

At laft we came to ourfelves, and faw him fitting in the porch looking at us ; when he had confidered us well, he advanced towards us, and, laying his hand upon me, he took me up by the nape of my neck, and turned me round as a butcher would do a fheep's-head ; after having viewed me well, and perceiving me to be fo lean that I had nothing but fkin and bone, he let me go. He took up all the reft, one by one, viewed them in the fame manner, and the captain being the fatteft, he held him with one hand, as I would do a fparrow, and thrufting a fpit thro' him, kindled a great fire, roafted, and ate him in his apartment for his fupper ; which being done, he returned to his porch, where he lay and fell afleep, fnoring louder than thunder : he flept thus till the morning ; for our part, it is not poffible for us to enjoy any reft, fo that we paffed the night in the moft cruel fear that can be

imagined.   Day being come, the giant awaked
got up, went out, and left us in the palace.

When we thought him at a diſtance, then we
broke the melancholy ſilence we had kept all
night, and every one grieving more than another, we made the palace to reſound with our
complaint and groans.   Though there was a
great many of us, and that we had but one enemy, we had not at firſt the preſence of mind to
think of delivering ourſelves from him by his
death.   This enterprize however, though hard
to put in execution, was the only deſign we
ought naturally to have formed.

We thought upon ſeveral other things, but
determined nothing ; ſo that ſubmitting to what
it ſhould pleaſe God to order concerning us, we
ſpent the day in running about the iſland, for
fruits and herbs to ſuſtain our lives.   When evening came, we ſought for a place to lie in, but
found none ; ſo that we were forced, whether we would or not, to return to the palace.

The giant failed not to come back, and ſup-

ped once more upon one of our companions ; after which he slept, and snored 'till day, and then
went out and left us as formerly.   Our condition
·was so very terrible, that several of my comrades
designed to throw themselves into the sea, rather than die so strange a death ; and those who
were of this mind, argued with the rest to follow
their example. Upon which, one of the company answered, that we were forbid to destroy ourselves ; but, allowing it to be lawful, it was
more reasonable to think of a way to rid ourselves
of the barbarous tyrant, who designed so cruel a
death for us.

Having thought of a project for that end, I
communicated the same to my comrades, who
improved it. " Brethren, said I, you know there
" is a great deal of timber floating upon the coast;
" if you will be advised by me, let us make seve-
" ral floats of it that may carry us, and when
" they are done, leave them there till we think
" fit to make use of them.   In the mean time,
" we will execute the design to deliver ourselves

" from the giant, and if it fucceed, we may
" ftay here with patience till fome fhip pafs by,
" that may carry us out of this fatal ifland ; but
" if it happen to mifcarry, we will fpeedily get
" to our floats, and put to fea. I confefs, that
" by expofing ourfelves to the fury of the waves
" we run a rifk of lofing our lives ; but if we
" do, is it not better to be buried in the fea, than
" in the entrails of this monfter, who has alrea-
" devoured two of us ?" My advice was relifhed,
and we made floats capable of carrying three perfons each.

We returned to the palace towards the evening, and the giant arrived a little while after.
We were forced to conclude on feeing another
of our comrades roafted. But at laft revenged
ourfelves on the brutifh giant thus. After he
had made an end of his curfed fupper, he lay
down on his back, and fell afleep. As foon as
we heard him fnore, according to his cuftom
nine of the boldeft among us, and myfelf, took
each of us a fpit and putting the points of them

into the fire till they were burning hot, we thruft them into his eye all at once, and blinded him. The pain occafioned him to make a frightful cry, and to get up and ftretch out his hands, in order to facrifice fome of us to his rage ; but we ran to fuch places as he could not find us, and after having fought for us in vain, he groped for the gate, and went our howling dreadfully.

We went out of the palace after the giant, and came to the fhore, where we had left our floats, and put them immediately into the fea. We waited till day, in order to get upon them in cafe the giant came towards us with any guide of his own fpecies ; but we hoped if he did not appear by fun-rifing, and gave over his howling, which we ftill heard, that he would die ; and if that happened to be the cafe, we refolved to ftay in that ifland, and not to rifk our lives upon the floats ; but day had fcarce appeared, till we perceived our cruel enemy, accompanied with two others almoft of the fame fize. leading him ; & a great number more coming before him, with a very quick pace.

When we ſaw this, we made no delay, but got immediately upon our floats, and rowed off from the ſhore. The Giants, who perceived this, took up great ſtones, and running to the ſhore, entered the water up to the middle, and threw ſo exactly, that they ſunk all the floats but that I was upon, and all my comrades, except the two with me, were drowned. We rowed with all our might, and got out of the reach of the giants. But when we got out to ſea, we were expoſed to the mercy of the waves and winds, and toſſed about ſometimes on one ſide, and ſometimes on another, and ſpent that night and the following day under a cruel uncertainty, as to our fate ; but next morning we had the good luck to be thrown upon an iſland, where we landed with much joy. We found excellent fruit there, that gave us great relief, ſo that we pretty well recovered our ſtrength.

In the evening we fell aſleep on the bank of

the fea, but were awaked by the noife of a ferpent as long as a palm-tree, whofe fcales made a
ruftling as he crept along.   He fwallowed up
one of my comrades, notwithftanding his loud
cries, and the efforts he made to rid himfelf from
the ferpent; which, after fhaking him feveral times againft the ground, crufhed him, and
we could hear him gnaw and tear the poor
wretch's bones, when we had fled at a great diftance from him.   Next day we faw the ferpent
again, to our great terror, when I cried out,
" O heaven, to what dangers are we expofed !
" We rejoiced yefterday at our having efcaped
" from the cruelty of a giant, and the rage of
" the waves, and now we are fallen into danger
" altogether as terrible".

As we walked about, we faw a large tall tree,
upon which we defigned to pafs the following
night for our fecurity ; and, having fatisfied our
hunger with fruit we mounted it accordingly.
A little while after, the ferpent came hiffing to
the root of the tree, raifed itfelf up againft the

D

trunk of it, and meeting with my comrade, who sat lower than I, swallowed him at once and went off.

I staid upon the tree till it was day and then came down, more like a dead man, than one alive, expecting the same fate with my two companions. This filled me with horror, so that I was going to throw myself into the sea ; but nature prompting us to a desire to live as long as we can, I withstood this temptation to despair, and submitted myself to the will of God, who disposes of our lives at his pleasure.

In the mean time I gathered together a great quantity of small wood, brambles, & dry thorns, and making them up in faggots, made a circle with them round the tree, and I also tied some to the branches over my head. Having done thus, when the evening came, I shut myself up within this circle, in order to preserve myself from the cruel destiny with which it was threatened. . The serpent failed not to come at the usual hour, and went round the tree, seeking for an opportunity to devour me, but was prevented by the rampart I had made ; so that he sat till day and then retired, but I dared not to leave my fort until the sun rose.

I was so fatigued with the toil the serpent had put me to, and suffered so much from his poisonous breath, that death seemed more eligible to me than the horror of such a condition. I came down from the tree ; and, not thinking on the resignation I had made to the will of God the preceeding day, I ran toward the sea, with a design to throw myself into it headlong.

God, however, took compassion on my desperate state : for just as I was going to throw myself into the sea, I perceived a ship at a considerable distance. I called as loud as I could, and taking the linen from my turban, displayed it, that they might observe me. This had the desired effect, all the crew perceived me, and the captain sent me his long-boat. As soon as I came aboard, the merchants and seamen flocked about me, to know how I came into that desart island ; and after I had told them all that befel me, the oldest . among them told me, they had several times heard of the giants who dwelt in that island that they were cannibals, and eat men raw as well as roasted ; and as to the serpents, they added, that there were abundance in the isle that hid themselves by day, and came abroad at night. After having testified their joy at my escaping so many dangers, they brought me the best of what they had to eat ; and the captain, seeing that I was all in rags, was so generous as to give me one of his own suits. We were at sea for some time, touched at several islands, and at last landed at that of Salabat, where there grows sanders, a wood of great use in physic. We entered the port, and came to an anchor the merchants began to unload their goods, in order to sell or exchange them. In the mean time the captain called to me and said, " Brother, I have here a parcel of goods that " belonged to a merchant, who sailed some " time on board this ship, and he being dead,

" I defign to difpofe of them for the benefit of
" his heirs, when I know them."   The bales
he fpoke of lay on the deck. and fhewing them
to me, he fays, " There are the goods.   I hope
" you will take care to fell them, and you fhall
" have factorage."   I thanked him that he gave
me an opportunity of employing myfelf, becaufe
I hated to be idle.

The clerk of the fhip took an account of all
the bales, with the names of the merchants to
whom they belonged.   And when he afked the
captain in whofe name he fhould enter thofe he
gave me the charge of ; " Enter them, fays the
" captain, in the name of Sindbad the Sailor."
I could not hear myfelf named without fome e-
motion, and looking ftedfaftly on the captain, I
knew him to be the perfon, who, in my fecond
voyage, had left me in the ifland where I fell a-
fleep by a brook, & fet fail without me, or fend-
ing to feek for me.   But I could not remember
him at firft, he was fo much altered fince I faw
him.

And as for him who believed me to be dead, I could not wonder at his not knowing me. " But " Captain, says I, was the merchant's name, to " whom those bales belonged, Sindbad? Yes, " replied he, that was his name; he came from " Bagdad, and embarked on board my ship at " Balsora. One day, when we landed at an i- " sland to take in water and other refreshments, " I know not by what mistake, I set sail with- " out observing that he did not reimbark with " us; neither I nor the merchants perceived it " till four hours after. We had the wind in our " stern, and so fresh a gale, that it was not pos- " sible for us to tack-about for him. " You " believe him then to be dead," says I, " cer- " tainly," answers he. " No Captain, says I, " look upon me, and you may know that I am " Sindbad, whom you left in that desart island; " I fell asleep by a brook, and when I awaked, " I found all the company gone."

The Captain, having looked at me attentively, knew me at last, embraced me, and said,

" God be praifed that Fortune has fupplied my
" defect.   There are your goods, which I al-
" ways took care to preferve ; and to make the
" beft of them at every port where I touched.
" I reftore them to you with the profit I have
" made of them."   I took them from him, and
at the fame time acknowledged how much I
owed to him.

From the ifle of Salabat we went to another,
where I furnifhed myfelf with cloves, cinnamon,
and other fpices.   As we failed from that ifland
we faw a tortoife that was 20 cubits in length
and breadth.   We obferved alfo, a fifh which
looked like a cow, and gave milk, and its fkin
is fo hard, that they ufually make bucklers of it.
I faw another which had the fhape and colour of
a camel.   In fhort, after a long voyage, I arrived at Balfora, and from thence returned to Bagdad, with fo much riches, that I knew not what
I had.   I gave a great deal of alms to the poor,
and bought another great eftate to what I had al-
ready.

SINDBAD

THE

FOURTH VOYAGE

OF

SINDBAD

THE

SAILOR.

———————◆◆◆———————

THE pleasures I took after my third voyage, had not charms enough to divert me from another. I was again prevailed upon by my passion for traffick, and curiosity to see new things, I therefore put my affairs in order, and having provided a stock of goods fit for the places where I designed to trade, I set out on my journey, . I took the way of Persia, of which I travelled several provinces, and then arrived at a port where

E

I embarked. We set sail, and having touched at several ports of Terra Firma, and some of the eastern islands, we put out to sea, and were seized by such a sudden gust of wind, as obliged the captain to furl his sails, and to make all other necessary precautions to prevent the danger that threatened us. But all was in vain, our endeavours took no effect, the sails were tore in a thousand pieces, and the ship was stranded, so that a great many of the merchants and seamen were drowned, and the cargo lost.

I had the good fortune, with several of the merchants and mariners, to get a plank, and we were carried by the current to an island which lay before us. There we found fruit and fountain-water, which preserved our lives. We staid all night a-shore, without consulting what we should do, our misfortune had dispirited us so much.

Next morning, as soon as the sun was up, we walked from the shore, and advancing into the islands, saw some houses, to which we went;

and as foon as we came thither, we were encompaffed by a great number of blacks, who
feized us, fhared us, among them, and carried
us to their refpective habitations.

I and five of my comrades were carried to one
place ; they made us fit down immediately, and
gave us a certain herb, which they made figns
for us to eat. My comrades not taking notice
that the blacks ate none of it themfelves con-
fulting only the fatisfying of their own hunger, fell
to eating with greedinefs. But I fufpecting
fome trick, would not fo much as tafte it, which
happened well for me ; for in a little time after,
I perceived my companions had loft their fenfes,
and that when they fpoke to me, they knew not
what they faid.

The blacks fed us afterwards with rice, prepared with oil of cocoas, & my comrades who had
loft their reafon, eat of it greedily. I eat of it
alfo, but very fparingly. The blacks gave us
that herb at firft on purpofe to deprive us of our
fenfes, that we might not be aware of the fad

deſtiny prepared for us ; and they gave us it on purpoſe to fatten us : for, being canibals, their deſign was to eat us as ſoon as we grew fat. They did accordingly eat my comrades who were not ſenſible of their condition ; but my ſenſes being intire, you may eaſily gueſs that inſtead of growing fat, as the reſt did, I grew leaner every day. The fear of death, under which I laboured, turned all my food into poiſon, I fell into a languiſhing diſtemper, which proved my ſafety ; for the blacks, having killed and eat up my companions, ſeeing me to be withered, lean and ſick, deferred my death till another time.

Mean while, I had a great deal of liberty, ſo that there was ſcarce any notice taken of what I did, and this gave me an opportunity one day to get at a diſtance from the houſes, and to make my eſcape. An old man, who ſaw me and ſuſpected my deſign, called to me as loud as he could to return ; but inſtead of obeying him I redoubled my pace, and quickly got out of ſight.

At that time there was none but the old man
about the houfes, the reft being abroad and not
to come home till night, which was pretty ufual
with them. Therefore, being fure that they
could not come time enough to purfue me, I
went on till night, then I ftopt to reft a little,
and to eat fome of the provifions I had taken
care for ; but I fpeedily fet forward again and
travelled feven days, avoiding thofe places which
feemed to be inhabited, and lived for the moft
part upon cocoa-nuts, which ferved me both for
meat and drink. On the eighth day I came near
the fea, and faw all of a fudden white people
like myfelf, gathering of pepper of which there
was great plenty in that place ; this I took to be
a good omen, and went to them without any
fcruple.

The people who gathered pepper came to
meet me as foon as they faw me, and afked me
in Arabic who I was, and whence I came ? I
was over-joyed to hear them fpeak in my own
language, and willingly fatisfied their curiofity

by giving them an account of my fhip-wreck, and how I fell into the hands of the blacks, Thofe blacks, replied they, eat men, and by what miracle did you efcape their cruelty ? I told them the fame ftory I now tell you, at which they were wonderfully furprized.

I ftaid with them till they had gathered their quantity of pepper, and then failed with them to the ifland from whence they came. They prefented me to their king, who was a good prince, he had the patience to hear the relation of my adventure, which furprized him ; and he afterwards gave me clothes, and commanded care to be taken of me.

The ifland was very well peopled, plentiful of every thing, and the capital was a place of great trade. This agreeable place of retreat was very comfortable to me after my misfortune, and the kindnefs of this generous prince towards me compleated my fatisfaction. In a word, there was not a perfon more in favour with him than myfelf, and in confequence every man in court and city fought how to oblige me ; fo that in a very little time I was looked upon rather as a native than a ftranger.

I obferved one thing which to me looked very extraordinary ; all the people, the king himfelf not excepted, rode their horfes without bridle or ftirrups.   This made me one day take the liberty to afk the king how that came to pafs? His majefty anfwered, that I talked to him of things which nobody knew the ufe of in his dominions.

I went immediately to a workman, and gave him a model for making the ftock of a faddle. When that was done, I covered it with leather, and embroidered it with gold.   I afterwards went to a lockfmith, who made me a bitt according to the pattern I fhewed him, and then he made alfo fome ftirrups.   When I had done, I prefented them to the king and put them upon one of his horfes.   His majefty mounted immediately, and was fo mightly pleafed with them, that he teftified his fatisfaction by large prefents to

me. I could not avoid making ſeveral others for
his miniſters and principal officers of his houſ-
hold, who all of them made me preſents that
enriched me in a little time. I alſo made for
the people of beſt quality in the city, which
gained me great reputation and regard from every
body.

As I made my court very exactly to the king
he ſays to me one day, " Sindbad, I love thee,
" and all my ſubjects who know thee treat thee
" according to my example. I have one thing
" to demand of thee, which thou muſt grant."
" Sir, anſwered I, there is nothing but what I
" will do, as a mark of my obedience to your
" majeſty, whoſe power over me is abſolute."
" I have a mind that thou ſhould'ſt marry, re-
" plies he, that ſo thou may'ſt ſtay in my domi-
" nions, and think no more of thy own coun-
" try." I dared not to reſiſt the prince's will,
and ſo he gave me one of the ladies of his court,
a noble, beautiful, chaſte, and rich lady. The
ceremonies of marriage being over, I went and

dwelt with the lady, and for fome time we lived together in perfect harmony. I was not, however, very well fatisfied with my condition, and therefore defigned to make my efcape on the firft occafion, and to return to Bagdad ; which my prefent fettlement, how advantageous foever, could not make me forget.

While I was thinking on this, the wife of one of my neighbours, with whom I had contracted a very ftrict friendfhip, fell fick and died. I went to fee and comfort him in his affliction, and finding him fwallowed up with forrow ; I faid to him as foon as I faw him, " God pre-
" ferve you, and grant you a long life." " A-
" las ! replies he, how do you think I fhould
" obtain that favour you wifh me ? I have not
" above an hour to live." " Pray, fays I,
" don't entertain fuch a melancholy thought,
" I hope it will not be fo, but that I fhall en-
" joy your company for many years." " I
" wifh you, fays he, a long life ; but for me,
" my days are at an end, for I muft be buried

" this day with my wife. This is a law which
" our anceftors eftablifhed in this ifland, and al-
" ways obferved it inviolably. The living huf-
" band is interred with the dead wife, and the
" living wife with the dead hufband. Nothing
" can fave me, every one muft fubmit to this
" law."

While he was entertaining me with an account
of this barbarous cuftom, the very hearing of
which frightened me cruelly, his kindred, friends,
and neighbours came in a body to affift a the funeral. They put on the corps the woman's
richeft apparel, as if it had been her wedding-
day, and dreffed her with all her jewels, then
they put her into an open coffin, and lifting it
up, began their march to the place of burial,
The hufband walked at the head of the company
and followed the corps. They went up to a high
mountain, and when they came thither, took up
a great ftone which covered the mouth of a very
deep pit, and let down the corps with all its apparel and jewels. Then the hufband, embracing

his kindred and friends, fuffered himfelf to be put into another open coffin without refiftance, with a pot of water, and feven little loves, and was let down in the fame manner they let down his wife. The mountain was pretty long, and reached to the fea. The ceremony being over they covered the hole again with the ftone and returned.

It is needlefs for me to tell you, that I was the only melancholy fpectator of this funeral, whereas the reft were fcarcely moved at it, the thing was fo cuftomary to them. I could not forbear fpeaking my thoughts of this matter to the king: " Sir, fays I, I cannot enough ex-
" prefs my wonder at the ftrange cuftom in this
" country, of burying the living with the dead
" I have been a great traveller, and feen many
" countries, but never heard of fo cruel a law."
" What do you mean, Sindbad, fays the king,
" it is a common law ? I fhall be interred with
" the queen, my wife, if fhe die firft," " But
" Sir, fays I, may I prefume to demand of your

" majefty, if ftrangers be obliged to obferve this
" law ?" " Without doubt, replied the king
" (fmiling at the occafion, of my queftion,) they
" are not excepted if they be married in this
" ifland."

I went home very melancholy at this anfwer ;
for the fear of my wife's dying firft, and that I
fhould be interred alive with her, occafioned me
to have very mortifying reflections.   But there
was no remedy, I muft have patience, and fubmit to the will of God.   I trembled however at
every little indifpofition of my wife ; but alas !
in a fhort time my fears came upon me all at
once, for fhe fell fick and died in a few days.

To be interred alive, feemed to me as deplorable an end, as to be devoured by canibals.
But I muft fubmit, the king and all his court
would honour the funeral with their prefence,
and the moft confiderable people of the city did
the like.   When all was ready for the ceremony
the corpfe was put into a coffin with all her jewels and magnificent apparel.   The cavalcade was

begun, and as second actor of this doleful trage-
dy, I went next the corpse, with my eyes full
of tears bewailing my deplorable fate. Before
I came to the mountain, I addressed myself to
the king in the first place, and then to all those
who were round me, and bowing before them to
the earth, to kifs the border of their garments,
I prayed them to have compassion upon me,
" Confider, said I, that I am a stranger, and
" ought not to be subject to this rigorous law,
" and that I have another wife and children in
" my own country." It was to no purpose for
me to speak thus, no soul was moved at it ; on
the contrary, they made hafte to let down my
wife's corpse into the pit, and put me down the
next moment in an open coffin, with a veffel full
of water, and seven loaves. In short the fatal
ceremony being performed they covered up the
mouth of the pit, notwithstanding the excess of
my grief, and my lamentable cries.

As I came near the bottom, I discovered, by
help of the little light that came from above the

nature of this subterranean place ; it was a vast long cave, and might be about 50 fathom deep. I immediately smelt an insufferable stench, proceeding from the multitude of dead corpses, which I saw on the right and left ; nay, I fancied that I heard some of them sigh out their last. However, when I got down, I immediately left my coffin, and getting at a distance from the corpse, held my nose, and lay down upon the ground, where I staid a long time bathed in tears. Then reflecting on my sad lot, " It is true, said I, " that God disposes all things according to the " decrees of his providence ; but, poor Sindbad, " art not thou thyself the cause of thy being " brought to die so strange a death ? Would to " God thou hadst perished in some of those tem- " pests which thou hadst escaped ! Then thy " death had not been so lingering, and terrible " in all its circumstances. But thou hast drawn " all this upon thyself by thy cursed avarice. " Ah ! unfortunate wretch ! Shouldst thou not

" rather have ftaid at home, and quietly enjoyed
" the fruit of thy labour."

Though the darknefs of the cave was fo great
that I could not diftinguifh day and night, yet I
always found my coffin again, and the cave feemed to be more fpacious, and fuller of corpfes than
it appeared to me at firft. I lived for fome days
upon my bread and water, which being all fpent
at laft I prepared for death.

As I was thinking of death, I heard the ftone
lifted up from the mouth of the cave, and immediately the corps of a man was let down.
When men are reduced to extremities, it is na-
tural for them to come to extreme refolutions.
While they let down the woman, I approached
the place where her coffin was to be put, and as
foon as I perceived they were covering again the
mouth of the cave, I gave the unfortune wretch
two or three great blows over the head, with a
bone that I found ; which ftunned, or, to fay
the truth, killed her. I committed this inhuman
action merely for the fake of the bread and water that was in her coffin, and thus I had provi-

fions for fome days more. When that was fpent, they let down another dead woman, and a live man ; I killed the man in the fame manner ; and, as good luck would have it for me, there was then a fort of morality in the town, fo that by this means I did not want for provifions.

One day, as I had difpatched another woman, I heard fomething walking, and blowing or panting as it walked. I advanced towards that fide from whence I heard the noife, and upon my approach the thing puffed and blew harder, as if it had been running away from me. I followed the noife, and the thing feemed to ftop fometimes, but always fled and blew as I approached. I followed it fo long, and fo far, till at laft I perceived a light, refembling a ftar ; I went on towards that light, and fometimes loft fight of it, but always found it again, and at laft difcovered that it came thro' a hole in the rock, large enough for a man to get out at.

Upon this, I ftopt fome time to reft myfelf, being much fatigued with purfuing this difcovery fo faft : afterwards coming up to the hole, I went out at it, and found myfelf upon the fea. I leave you to guefs at the excefs of my joy ; it was fuch that I could fcaree perfuade myfelf of its being real.

But when I was recovered from my furprize, and convinced of the truth of the matter, I found the thing which I had followed, and heard puff and blow, to be a creature which came out of the fea, and was accuftomed to en'er at that hole to feed upon dead carcafes.

I confidered the mountain, and perceived it to be fituated betwixt the fea and the town, but without any paffage or way to communicate with the latter, the rocks on the fide of the fea, were fo rugged and fteep.   I fell down upon the fhore to thank God for his mercy, and afterwards entered the cave again to fetch bread and water, which I did eat by day-light with a better appetite than I had done fince my interment in the dark hole.

I returned thither again, and groped about a-

F

mong the biers for all the diamonds, rubies, pearls, gold, bracelets, and rich stuffs I could find ; these I brought to the shore, and tying them up neatly into bales, with the cords that let down the coffins, I laid them together upon the bank, waiting till some ship passed, by, without any fear of rain, for it was not then the season.

· After two or three days I perceived a ship that had but just come out of the harbour, and passed near the place where I was. I made a sign with the linen of my turban, & called to them as loud as I could : they heard me, and sent a sloop to bring me on board. When the mariners asked by what misfortune I came thither ? I told them that I suffered shipwreck two days ago, and made shift to get ashore with the goods they saw. It was happy for me that those people did not consider the place where I was, nor enquire into the probability of what I told them ; but without any more ado, took me on board with my goods. When I came to the ship, the captain was so well pleased to have saved me, and so much taken up with his own affairs, that he alſo took the ſtory of my pretended ſhipwreck upon truſt, and generouſly refuſed ſome jewels which I offered him.

We paſſed by ſeveral iſlands, and among others, that called Serendib, with a regular wind, and ſix leagues from that of Kela, where we landed. This iſland produces lead-mines, Indian canes, and excellent camphire.

The king of the iſle of Kela is very rich and potent ; and the iſle of Bells, which is about two days journey in extent, is alſo ſubject to him. The inhabitants are ſo barbarous, that they ſtill eat human fleſh. After we had finiſhed our commerce in that iſland, we put to ſea again, and touched at ſeveral other ports ; at laſt I arrived happily at Bagdad with infinite riches, of which it is needleſs to trouble you with the detail. Out of thankfulneſs to God for his mercies, I gave great alms for the entertainment of ſeveral moſques, and for the ſubſiſtence of the poor, and employed myſelf wholly in enjoying my kindred and friends.

F 2

SINDBAD

THE

FIFTH VOYAGE

OF

SINDBAD

THE

SAILOR.

THE pleaſures I enjoyed had again charms enough to make me forget all the troubles ancalamities I had undergone, without curing me of my inclination to make new voyages. Therefore I bought goods, ordered them to be packed up, and loaded, and ſet out with them for the beſt ſea-port, and there, that I might not be obliged to depend upon a captain, but have a ſhip at my own command, I ſtaid tlll one was built on purpose, at my own charge. When the ship was ready, I went on board with my goods; but not having enough to load her, I took on board me several merchants of different nations with their merchandize.

We sailed with the first fair wind, and after a long navigation, the first place we touched at was a desart island, where we found an egg of a roc, equal in bigness with that I formerly mentioned. There was a young roc in it just ready to be hatched, and the bill of it began to appear.

The merchants, whom I had taken on board my ship, and who landed with me, broke the egg with hatchets, and made a hole in it, from whence they pulled out the young roc piece after piece, and roasted it. I had earnestly dissuaded them from meddling with the egg, but they would not listen to me.

Scarce had they made an end of their treat, when there appeared in the air, at a confiderable distance from us, two great clouds. The capᵗain, whom I hired to fail my ſhip, knowing by experience what it meant, cried that it was the he and ſhe roc that belonged to the young one, and preſſed us to reimbark with all ſpeed, to prevent the misfortune which we ſaw would otherwiſe befall us, We made haſte to do ſo-and ſet ſail with all poſſible diligence.

In the mean time the two rocs approached with a frightful noiſe, which they redoubled when they ſaw the egg broke, and their young one gone. But having a mind to avenge them-ſelves, they flew back towards the place from whence they came, and diſappeared for ſome time, while we made all the ſail we could, to prevent that which unhappily befel us.

They returned, and we obſerved that each of them carried betwixt their talons, ſtones, or ra-ther rocks of monſtrous ſize. When they came directly over my ſhip, they hovered, and one of them let fall a ſtone, but by the dexterity of the ſteerſman, who immediately turned the ſhip with the rudder, it miſſed us, and falling by the fide of the fhip into the fea, divided the water fo, that we almoft could fee to the bottom. The other roc, to our misfortune, threw the ftone fo exactly upon the middle of the fhip, that it fplit in a thoufand pices. The mariners and paffengers were all killed by the ftone, or funk. I myfelf had the laft fate ; but as I came up again, I catched hold by good fortune of a piece of the wreck, and fwimming fometimes with one hand and fometimes with the other, but always holding faft my board, the wind and tide being for me, I came to an ifland whofe bank was very fteep. I overcome that difficulty, however, and got afhore.

I fat down upon the grafs, to recover myfelf a little from my fatigue, after which I got up and went into the ifland to view it. It feemed to be a delicious garden. I found trees every where, fome of them bearing green, and others ripe fruits, and ftreams of frefh pure water, with pleafant windings and turnings. I ate of the fruits, which I found excellent ; and drank of the water, which was very pleafant.

Night being come, I lay down upon the grafs, in a place convenient enough, but I could not fleep an hour at a time, my mind was fo difturbed with the fear of being alone in fo defart a place. Thus I fpent the beft part of the night in fretting, and reproaching myfelf for my imprudence in not ftaying at home, rather than undertaking this laft voyage. But day-light difperfed thofe melancholy thoughts, and I got up and walked among the trees, but not without apprehenfions of danger.

When I was a little advanced into the ifland I faw an old man, who to me feemed very weak and feeble. He fat upon the bank of a ftream, and at firft I took him to be one who had been fhipwrecked like myfelf. I went towards him, and faluted him, but he only bowed his head a little. I afked him what he did there, but inftead of anfwering me, he made a fign for me to take him upon my back, and carry him over

. G

the brook, fignifying that it was to gather fruit.

I believed him really to ftand in need of my help, fo took him upon my back, and having carried him over, bid him get down, and for that end I ftooped, that he might get off with eafe ; but inftead of that, (which makes me laugh at every time I think on't) the old man, who to me appeared very decrepid, clafped his legs nimbly about my neck, and then I perceived his fkin to refemble that of a cow. He fat aftride upon my fhoulders, and held my throat fo ftrait, that I thought he would have ftrangled me, the fright of which made me faint away and fall down.

Notwithftanding my fainting, the ill-natured old follow kept faft about my neck, but opened his legs a little to give me time to recover my breath. When I had done fo, he thruft one of his feet againft my ftomach, and ftruck me fo rudely on the fide with the other, that he forced me to rife up againft my will. Being got up, he made me walk under the trees, and forced me now and then to ftop, to gather and eat fuch fruit as we found. He never left me all day, and when I lay down to reft me by night, he laid himfelf down with me, holding always faft about my neck. Every morning he pufhed me, to make me awake, and afterwards obliged me to get up and walk, and preffed me with his feet. You may judge then what trouble I was in, to be charged with fuch a burden as I could no ways rid myfelf from.

One day I found in my way feveral dry cale-bafhes, that had fallen from a tree; I took a large one, and, after cleaning it, preffed into it fome juice of grapes, which abounded in the ifland; having filled the calebafh, I fet it in a convenient place, and coming hither again fome days after, I took up my calebafh, and fetting it to my mouth, found the wine to be fo good, that it made me prefently not only forget my forrow, but I grew fo vigorous, and was fo light-hearted that I began to fing and dance as I walked along.

The old man perceiving the effect which this

drink had upon me, and that I carried him with
more eaſe than I did before, made a ſign for me
give him ſome of it. I gave him the calebaſh
and the liquor pleaſing his palate, he drank it all
off. There being enough of it to fuddle him, he
became drunk immediately, and the fumes getting up into his head, he began to ſing after his
manner, and to dance with his breech upon my
ſhoulders. His jolting about made me vomit,
and he looſened his legs from about me by de-
grees ; ſo finding that he did not preſs me as before, I threw him upon the ground, where he
lay without motion, and then I took up a great
ſtone, with which I cruſhed his head to pieces.

I was extremely rejoiced, to be freed thus
from this curſed old fellow, and walked upon
the bank of the ſea, where I met the crew of a
ſhip that had caſt anchor, to take in water and
refreſh themſelves. They were extremely ſurprized to ſee me, and to hear the particulars
of my adventures. You fell, ſaid they, into the
hands of the old man of the ſea, and are the firſt

, that ever efcaped ftrangling by him. He never left thofe he had once made himfelf mafter of, till he deftroyed them, and he has made this iíland famous by the number of men he has flain fo that the merchants and mariners who landed upon it, dared not to advance into the ifland, but in numbers together.

After having informed me of thofe things, they earried me with them to the fhip, the captain received me with great fatisfaction, when they told him what had befallen me. He put out again to fea, and after fome days fail, we arrived at the harbour of a great city, whofe houfes were built with good ftone.

One of the merchants of the fhip, who had taken me into his friendfhip, obliged me to go along with him, and carried me to a place appointed for a retreat for foreign merchants. He gave me a great bag, and having recommended me to fome people of the town, who ufed to gather cocoas, he defired them to take me with them to do the like ; " Go fays he, follow

" them, and do as you fee them do, and don't
" feparate from them, otherwife you endanger
" your life". Having thus fpoke, he gave me
provifions for the journey, and I went with
them.

We came to a great foreft of trees, extremely
ftrait and tall, and their trunks were fo fmooth,
that it was not poffible for any man to climb up
to the branches, that bore the fruit. All the
trees were cocoa-trees, and when we entered the
foreft we faw a great number of apes of feveral
fizes, that fled as foon as they perceived us, and
climbed up to the tops of the trees with furprizing fwiftnefs.

The merchants with whom I was, gathered,
ftones, and threw them at the apes on the tops
of the trees. I did the fame, and the apes out
of revenge threw cocoa-nuts at us as faft, and
with fuch geftures as fufficiently teftified their an-
ger and refentment ; we gathered up the cocoas,
and from time to time threw ftones to provoke
the apes ; fo that by this ftratagem we filled our

bags with cocoa-nuts, which it had been impoffible for us to have done otherwife.   -

When we had gathered our number, we returned to the city, where the merchant who fent
me to the foreft, gave me the value of the cocoas, I brought : " Go on, fays he, and do the
" like every day until you have got money e-
" nough to carry you home." I thanked him
for his good advice, and infenfibly gathered together fo many cocoas as mounted to a confiderable fum.

The veffel in which I came, failed with merchants who loaded her with cocoas. I expected
the arrival of another, which landed fpeedily for
the like loading. I embarked on board the fame
all the cocoas that belonged to me. and when fhe
was ready to fail, I went and took leave of the
merchant, who had been fo kind to me ; but he
could not embark with me, becaufe he had not
finifhed his affairs.

We fet fail towards the ifland, where pepper
grows in great plenty. From thence we went

to the isle of Comari, where the best sort of
wood of aloes grows, and whose inhabitants have
made it an inviolable law to themselves, to drink
no wine, nor suffer any place of debauch.   I exchanged my cocoas in those two islands, for pepper and wood of aloes, and went with other merchants a pearl-fishing, I hired divers, who fetch-
ed me up those that were very large and pure.
I embarked joyfully on a vessel that arrived happily at Balsora ; from thence I returned to Bagdad, where I made vast sums of my pepper, wood
of aloes and pearls.   I gave the tenth of my gain
in alms, as I had done upon my return from
other voyages, and endeavoured to ease myself
from my fatigues, by diversions of all sorts .

SINDBAD

SINDBAD

THE

SAILOR.

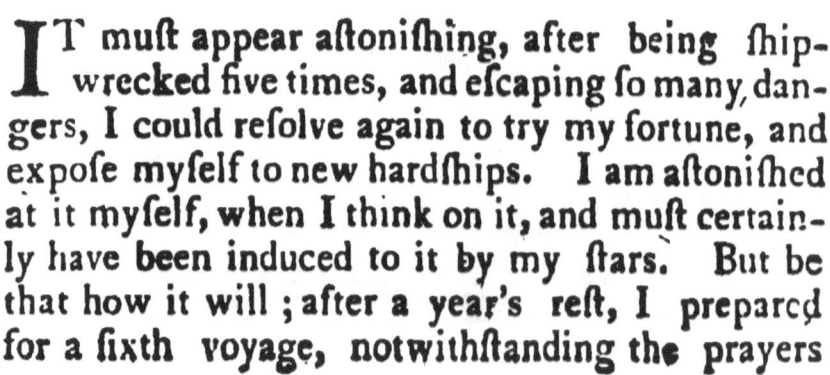

I T muſt appear aſtoniſhing, after being ſhip-
wrecked five times, and eſcaping ſo many, dangers, I could reſolve again to try my fortune, and
expoſe myſelf to new hardſhips. I am aſtoniſhed
at it myſelf, when I think on it, and muſt certain-
ly have been induced to it by my ſtars. But be
that how it will ; after a year's reſt, I prepared
for a ſixth voyage, notwithſtanding the prayers

of my kindred and friends, who did all that was possible to prevent me.

Instead of taking my way by the Persian gulph I travelled once more thro' several provinces of Persia and the Indies, and arrived at a sea-port, where I embarked on board a ship, the captain of which was resolved on a long voyage.

It was very long indeed, but at the same time so unfortunate, that the captain and pilot lost their course, so as they knew not where they were. They found it at last, but we had no ground to rejoice at it. We were all seized with extraordinary fear, when we saw the captain quit his post, and cry out. He threw off his turban, pulled the hair off his beard, and beat his head like a madman. We asked him the reason and he answered, that he was in the most dangerous place of all the sea. A rapid current carries the ship along with it, and we shall all of us perish in less than a quarter of an hour. Pray to God, to deliver us from this danger, we cannot escape it, if he don't take pity on us.

At thefe words he ordered the fails to be changed,—but all the ropes broke, and the fhip, without being poffible to help it, was carried by the current to the foot of an unacceffible mountain, where fhe was run afhore and broke to pieces, yet fo as we faved our lives, our provifions, and the beft of our goods.

This being over, the captain fays to us, " God has now done what he pleafed, we may every man dig our grave here, and bid the world adieu, for we are in fo fatal a place, that none fhipwrecked here did ever return to their homes again." His difcourfe afflicted us mortally, and we embraced one another with tears in our eyes bewailing our deplorable lot.

The mountain at the foot of which we were caft, was the coaft of a very long and large ifland. This coaft was covered all over with wrecks, and by the vaft number of men's bones we faw every where, and which filled us with horror, we concluded that abundance of people had died there. It is alfo incredible to tell, what a quantity of goods and riches we found cast ashore there. All those objects served only to augment our grief. Whereas in all other places, rivers run from their channels into the sea, here a great river of fresh water runs out of the sea into a dark cave, whose entrance is very high and large. What is most remarkable in this place is, that the stones of the mountain are of chrystal, rubies or other precious stones. Here is also a sort of a fountain of pitch or bitumen, that runs into the sea, which the fishes swallow, and then vomit up again turned into ambergrease ; and this the waves throw upon the beach in great quantities. Here grows also trees, most of which are of wood of aloes, equal in goodness to those of Camari.

To finish the description of this place, which may well be called a gulph, since nothing ever returns from it, it is not possible for a ship to get off from it, when once they come within such a distance of it. If they be drove thither by a wind from the sea, the wind and the current ruins them ; & if they come into it when a land wind blows, which might feem to favour their getting out again, the height of the mountain ftops the wind and occafions a calm, fo that the force of the current runs them afhore, where they are broke in pieces, as ours was ; and that which compleats the misfortune, is, that there is no pof-fibility to get to the top of the mountain, or to get out any manner of way.

We continued upon the fhore, like men out of their fenfes, and expected death every day. At firft we divided our provifions as equally as we could, and fo every one lived a longer or a fhorter while, according to their temper, and the ufe they made of their provifions.

Thofe who died firft were interred by the reft ; and as for my part, I paid the laft duty to all my companions : nor are you to wonder at this ; for I hufbanded the provifion that fell to my fhare better than they ; yet when I buried the laft, I had fo little remaining, that I thought I could not hold out any longer. So that I digged a grave, refolving to lie down in it, becaufe there was none left alive to inter me. I muft confefs to you at the fame time, that while I was thus employed, I could not but reflect upon my unconquerable fpirit for travelling, as the caufe of my own ruin.

But it pleafed God once more to take compaffion on me, and put in my mind to go to the bank of the river which runs into the great cave, where confidering the river with great attention, I faid to myfelf, " This river, which runs thus " under ground, muft come out fomewhere or " other. If I make a float, and leave myfelf to " the current, Providence may bring me to fome " inhabited country, where I may, perhaps " find fome new occafion of enriching myfelf.

After this, I immediately went to work on a float, I made it of good large pieces of timber and cables, for I had choice of them, and tied them together fo ftrong, that I had made a very folid little float. When I had finifhed it, I loaded it with fome bales of rubies, emeralds, ambergreaſe, roc-cryſtal, and rich ſtuffs. Having balanced my cargo exactly, and faſtened it well to the float, I went on board it with two little oars that I had made, and leaving it to the courſe of the river, I reſigned myſelf to the will of God.

As ſoon as I came into the cave, I loſt all light, and the ſtream carried me I know not whither. Thus I ſailed ſome days in perfect darkneſs, and once found the arch ſo low, that it well nigh broke my head, which made me very cautious afterwards of avoiding the like danger. All this while I ate nothing but what was juſt neceſſary to ſupport nature ; yet notwithſtanding this frugality, all my proviſions were ſpent. Then a pleaſant ſleep ſeized upon me. I cannot tell how long it continued ; but which I awaked, I was ſurprized to find myſelf in the middle of a vaſt country, at the brink of a river, where my float was tied, amidſt a great number of negroes. I got up as ſoon as I ſaw them, and ſaluted them. They ſpoke to me, but I did not underſtand their language.

One of the blacks who underſtood Arabic,
hearing me ſpeak in that language, came toward
me, and ſaid, " Brother, don't be ſurprized to
" ſee us, we are inhabitants of this country, and
" came hither to-day to water our fields, by dig-
" ging little canals from this river, which comes
" out of the neighbouring mountain.   We per-
" ceived ſomething floating upon the water, went
" ſpeedily to ſee what it was, and perceiving
" your float, one of us ſwam into the river and
" brought it hither, where we faſtened it, as you
" ſee, until you ſhould awake.   Pray tell us your
" hiſtory, for it muſt be extraordinary ; how did
" you venture yourſelf into this river, and whence
" do you come ?" I begged of them firſt to give
me ſomething to eat, and then I would ſatisfy
their curioſity.   They gave me ſeveral ſorts of
food, and when I had ſatisfied my hunger, I gave
them a true account of all that had befallen me,
which they liſtened to with admiration.   As ſoon
as I had finiſhed my diſcourſe, they told me by
the perſon who ſpoke Arabic, and interpreted
H

to them what I faid, that it was one of the moft furprizing ftories they ever heard, and that I muft go along with them, and tell it their king myfelf; the thing was too extraordinary to be told him by any other than the perfon to whom it happened. I told them I was ready to do whatever they pleafed.

They immediately fent for a horfe, which was brought them in a little time, and having made me get up upon him, fome of them walked before me to fhew me the way, and the reft took my float and cargo, and followed me.

We marched thus altogether, till we came to the city of Serendib, for 'twas in that ifland where I landed. The blacks prefented me to their king, I approached his throne, and faluted him as I ufed to do the kings of the Indies; that is to fay, I proftrated myfelf at his feet, and kiffed the earth. The prince ordered me to rife up, received me with an obliging air, and made me come up, and fit down near him. He firft afked me my name, and I anfwered Sindbad the

Sailor, becaufe of the many voyages I had un-
dertaken, and that I was a citizen of Bagdad.
" But, replies he, how did you come into my
" dominions, and from whence came you laft."

I concealed nothing from the king ; I told
him all that I have now told you, and his majefty was fo furprized and charmed with it, that
he commanded my adventures to be writ in let-
ters of gold, and laid up in the archives of his
kingdom. At laft my float was brought him,
and the bales opened in his prefence ; he admired the quantity of wood of aloes, and amber-
greafe, but above all, the rubies and emeralds,
for he had none in his treafury that came near
them.

Obferving that he looked on my jewels with
pleafure, and viewed the moft remarkable among
them, one after another, I fell proftrate at his
feet, and took the liberty to fay to him, " Sir,
" not only my perfon is at your majefty's fervice;
" but the cargo of the float, and I beg of you to
" difpofe of it as your own " He anfwered me

with a fmile, " Sindbad, I will take care not to
" covet any thing of yours, nor to take any
" thing from you that God has given you; far
" from leffening your wealth, I defign to aug-
" ment it, and will not let you go out of my
" dominions without marks of my liberality."
All the anfwer I returned was prayers for the
profperity of that prince, and commendations of
his generofity and bounty.   He charged one of
his officers to take care of me, and ordered people to ferve me at his own charge.   The officer
was very faithful in the execution of his orders,
and made all the goods to be carried to the lodg-
ings provided for me.

I went every day at a fet hour to make my
court to the king, and fpent the reft of my time
in feeing the city, and what was moft worthy of
my curiofity.

The Ifle of Serendib is fituated juft under the
equinoctial line; fo that the days and night there
are always of twelve hours each, and the ifland

is eighty parafangues in length, and as many in
breadth.

The capital city ftands in the end of a fine valley, formed by a mountain, in the middle of the
ifland, which is the higheft in the world.   It is
feen three days fail at fea.   There are rubies
and feveral forts of minerals in it, and all the
rocks for the moft part emerald, a metallic ftone
made ufe of to cut and fmooth other precious
ftones.   There is alfo a pearl-fifhing in the
mouth of its river ; and in fome of its vallies
there are found diamonds.

I prayed the King to allow me to return to my
country, which he granted me in the moft obliging and moft honourable manner.   He would
needs force a rich prefent upon me ; and when
I went to take my leave of him, he gave me one
much more confiderable, and at the fame time
charged me with a letter for the Commander of
the Faithful our Sovereign Lord, faying to me,
" I pray you give this prefent from me, and
" this letter to Caliph Haroun Alrafchid, and

" affure him of my friendfhip." I took the prefent and letter in a very refpectful manner, and promifed his majefty punctually to execute the commands with which he was pleafed to honour me. Before I embarked, this prince fent to feek for the captain and the merchants that were to go with me, and ordered them to treat me with all poffible refpect.

The letter from the King of Serendib was wrote on the fkin of a certain animal of great value, becaufe of its being fo fcarce, and of a yellowifh colour. The characters of this letter were of azure, and the contents thus.

The King of the Indies, before whom march 100 Elephants, who lives in a Palace that fhines 100000 Rubies, and who has in his Treafury 20000 Crowns enriched with Diamonds, to Caliph Haroun Alrafchid.

THOUGH the Prefent we fend you be inconfiderable, receive it however as a Brother and a

Friend, in consideration of the hearty Frendship which we hear for you, and of which we are willing to give you Proof. We desire the same Part in your Friendship, considering that we believe it to be our merit, being of the same Dignity with yourself, We conjure you this in Quality of a Brother, Adieu.

The present consisted in the first place, of one single ruby made into a cup, about half a foot high, an inch thick, and filled with round pearls of half a dram each. 2. Of the skin of a serpent, whose scales were as large as an ordinary piece of gold, and had the virtue to preserve from sickness those who lay upon it. 3. In 50000 drams of the best wood aloes, with 30 grains of camphire as big as pistachio nuts. And 4. A she-slave of ravishing beauty, whose apparel was all covered over with jewels.

The ship, set sail, and after a long and very successful voyage, we landed at Balsora, from whence I went to Bagdad, where the firſt thing I did was to acquit myſelf of my commiſſion.

I took the King of Serendib's letter, and went to preſent myſelf at the gate of the Commander of the Faithful, followed by the beautiful ſlave, and ſuch of my own family as carried the preſents. I gave an account of the reaſon of my coming, and was immediately conducted to the throne of the Caliph. I made my reverence by proſtration, and, after a ſhort ſpeech, gave him the letter and preſent. When he had read what the King of Serendib wrote to him, he aſked me, if that prince were really ſo rich and potent as he had ſaid in his letter?

I proſtrated myſelf a ſecond time, and riſing again, "Commander of the Faithful, ſays I, I "can aſſure your majeſty he doth not exceed the "truth on that head, I am a witneſs of it. "There is nothing more capable of raiſing a "man's admiration, that the magnificence of "his palace. And further, the King of Seren- "dib is ſo juſt, that there are no judges in his

" dominions. His people have no need of them.
" They underſtand and obſerve juſtice exactly of
" themſelves." The Caliph was much pleaſed
" with my diſcourſe." The wiſdom of that
" king, ſays he, appears in his letter, and after
" what you tell me, I muſt confeſs, that his
" wiſdom is worthy of his people, and his peo-
" ple deſerve ſo wiſe a prince. Having ſpoke
" thus, he diſcharged me, and ſent me home
" with a rich preſent.

I

SEVENTH VOYAGE

OF

S I N D B A D

THE

SAILOR.

━━━━━◉━━━━━

BEING returned from my fixth voyage, I absolutely laid afide all my thoughts of travelling any farther. For, befides that my years did now require reft, I was refolved no more to expofe myfelf to fuch rifks as I had run. So that I thought of nothing but to pafs the reft of my days in quiet. One day as I was treating a parcel of my friends, one of my fervants came and told me, that an officer of the Caliph's afked for me. I rofe from the table, and went to him. " The Caliph, fays he, has fent me to " tell you, that he muft fpeak with you." I fol- lowed the officer to the palace, where being pre- fented to the Cal:ph, I faluted him by proftrat- ing myfelf at his feet. " Sindbad, fays he to " me, I ftand in need of you, you muft do me " the fervice to carry my anfwer and prefent to " the King of Serendib. It is but juft I fhould " return his civility."

This command of the Caliph to me was like a clap of thunder. "Commander of the Faith- " ful, replied I, I am ready to do whatever " your majefty fhall think fit to command me " but I befeech you moft humbly to confider " what I have undergone. I have alfo made a " vow never to go out of. Bagdad." Hence I took occafion to give him a large and particular accuunt of all my adventures, which he had the patience to hear out.

As foon as I had finifhed, " I confefs, fays " he, that the things you tell me are very ex-

I 2

" traordinary, yet you muſt for my ſake under-
" take this voyage which I propoſe to you.
" You have nothing to do but to go to the iſle
" of Serendib, and deliver the commiſſion which
" I give you. After that, you are at liberty
" to return. But you muſt go, for you
" know it would be undecent, and not ſuita-
" ble to my dignity, to be indebted to the
" King of that iſland." Perceiving that the Caliph inſiſted upon it, I ſubmitted, and told him
that I was willing to obey. He was very well
pleaſed at it, and ordered me 1000 ſequins for
the charge of my journey.

I prepared for my departure in a few days,
and as ſoon as the Caliph's letter and preſent
were delivered to me, I went to Balſora, where
I embarked, and had a very happy voyage. I
arrivd at the iſle of Serendib, where I acquainted, the King's miniſters with my commiſſion, and
prayed them to get me ſpeedy audience. They
did ſo, and was conducted to the palace in an
honourable manner, where I ſaluted the King

by proftration, according to cuftom. That
prince knew me immediately, and teftified very
great joy to fee me. " O Sindbad, fays he,
" you are welcome, I fwear to you I have ma-
" ny times thought of you fince you went from
" hence, I blefs the day upon which we fee one
" another once more." I made my compliment
to him, and, after having thanked him for his
kindnefs to me, I delivered him the Caliph's letter and prefent, which he received with all ima-
ginable fatisfaction.

The Caliph's prefent was a compleat bed of
cloth of gold, valued at 1000 fequins. Fifty
robes of rich ftuff, a hundred others of white
cloth, another crimfon bed, and a third of another fafhion. A veffel of agate, broader than
deep, of an inch thick, and half a foot wide,
the bottom of which reprefented in bafs-relief, a
man with one knee on the ground, who held a
bow and arrow, ready, to let fly at a lion. He
fent him alfo a rich table, which according to

I 3

tradition, belonged to the great Solomon.   The Caliph's letter was as follows ;

Greeting in Name of the Sovereign Guide of the Right Way, to the Potent and Happy Sultan, from Abdallah Haroun Alrafchid, whom God hath fet in the Place of Honour, after his Anceftors of happy Memory.

WE received your Letter with Joy, and fend you this from the Council of our Port ; the Garden of fuperior Wits.   We hope when you look upon it you will find our good Intention, and be pleafed with it.   Adieu.

The King of Serendib was mightly pleafed that the Caliph anfwered his friendfhip.   A little time after this audience, I folicited leave to depart and obtained the fame with much difficulty.

I got it however at laft, and the King, when he difcharged me, made me a very confiderable

prefent.   I embarked immediately to return to
Bagdad, but had not the good fortune to arrive
there as I hoped.   God ordered it otherwife.

Three or four days after my departure, we
were attacked by Corfairs, who eafily feized
upon our fhip, becaufe it was no veffel of force.
Some of the crew offered refiftance, which coft
them their lives.   But for me and the reft, who
were not fo imprudent, the Corfairs faved us on
purpofe to make flaves of us.

We were all ftript, and inftead of our own
cloaths, they gave us forry rags, and carried us
into a remote ifland, where they fold us.

I fell into the hands of a rich merchant, who
as foon as he bought me, carried me to his houfe,
treated me well, and clad me handfomely for a
flave.   Some days after, not knowing what I
was, he afked me if I underftood any trade ; I
anfwered, that I was no mechanic, but a merchant, and that the Corfairs, who fold me, rob-
bed me of all I had.   " But tell me, " replies
he, "can you fhoot with a bow ?" I anfwered,

I 4

" That the bow was one of the exercifes of my
" youth, and I had not yet forgot it." Then
he gave me a bow and arrows, and, with a drefs
peculiar to the ifland, carried me to a vaſt foreſt
fome leagues from the town.   We went a great
way into the foreſt, and when he thought fit to
ftop, he bid me alight ; then, fhewing me a
great tree, " Climb up that tree," fays he,
" and fhoot at the elephants as you fee them
" pafs by, for there is a prodigious number of
" them in this foreſt, and if any of them fall
" come and give me notice of it." Having
fpoke thus, he left me victuals, and returned to
the town, and I continued upon the tree all the
night.

I faw no elephant during that time, but next
morning, as foon as the fun was up, I faw a
great number ; I fhot feveral arrows among them
and at laſt one of the elephants fell ; the reſt retired immediately, and left me at liberty to go
and acquaint my patron with my booty, when I
told him the news, he gave me a good meal,

commended my dexterity, and careffed me migh-tily. We went afterwards together to the foreft, where we dug a hole for the elephant ; my pa-tron defigning to return when it was rotten, and to take his teeth, &c. to trade with.

I continued this game for two months, and killed an elephant every day, getting fometimes upon one tree and fometimes upon another. One morning, as I looked for the elephants, I per-ceived with an extreme amazement, that, in-ftead of paffing by me a-crofs the foreft as ufual they ftopped and came to me with a horrible noife, in fuch number that the earth was cover-ed with them, and fhook under me. They encompaffed the tree where I was, with their trunks extended, and their eyes all fixed upon me. At this frightful fpectacle I continued un-moveable, and was fo much frightened, that my bow and arrows fell out of my hand.

My fears were not in vain ; for after the ele-phants had ftared upon me fome time, one of the largeft of them put his trunk round the root of the tree, and pulled fo ftrong, that he plucked it up, and threw it on the ground ; I fell with the tree, and the elephant taking me up with his trunk, laid me on his back, where I fat more like one dead than alive, with my quiver on my fhoulder : he put himfelf afterwards at the head of the reft, who followed him in troops, and carried me to a place where he laid me down on the ground, and retired with all his companions. Conceive, if you can, the condition I was in : I thought myfelf to be in a dream ; at laft, after having laid fome time, and feeing the elephants gone, I got up and found I was upon a long and broad hill, covered all over with the bones and teeth of elephants. I confefs to you, that this object furnifhed me with abundance of reflections. I admired the inftinct of thofe animals ; I doubted not but that was their burying-place, and that they carried me thither on purpofe to tell me that I fhould forbear to perfecute them, fince I did it only for their teeth. I did not ftay on the hill, but turned towards the city, and, after having

travelled a day and a night, I came to my patron ;
I met no elephant in my way, which made me
think they retired father into the foreft, to leave
me at liberty to come back to the hill without
any obftacle.

As foon as my patron faw me, "Ah, poor
" Sindbad," fays he, " I was in great trouble to
" know what was become of you. I have been
" at the foreft, where I found a tree newly pull-
" ed up, and a bow and arrows on the ground,
" and after having fought for·you in vain, I
" defpaired of ever feeing you more. Pray tell
" me what befel you, and by what good hap thou
" art ftill alive." I fatisfied his curiofity, and,
going both of us next morning to the hill, he
found, to his great joy, that what I told him was
true. We loaded the elephant upon which we
came, with as many teeth as he could carry ; and
when we were returned, " Brother," fays my pa-
" tron, " for I will treat you no more as a flave.
" after having made fuch a difcovery as will en-
" rich me. God blefs you with all happinefs &

" profperity. I declare before him, that I give
" you your liberty. I concealed from you what
" I am now going to tell you.

" The elephants of our foreft have killed us a
" great many flaves, whom we fent to feek ivory.
" For all the cautions we could give them, thofe
" crafty animals killed them one time or other.
" God has delivered you from their fury, and has
" beftowed that favour upon you only. It is
" a fign that he loves you, and has ufe for your
" fervice in the world. You have procured me
" incredible gain. We could not have ivory,
" formerly, but by expofing the lives of our
" flaves ; and now our whole city is enriched by
" your means. Do not think I pretend to have
" rewarded you by giving you your liberty,
" I will alfo give you confiderable riches. I
" could engage all our city to contribute towards
" making your fortune, but I will have the glo-
" ry of doing it alone.

To this obliging difcourfe I replied, " Patron,
" God preferve you. Your giving me my liber-

" ty is enough to difcharge what you owe me,
" and I defire no other reward for the fervice I
" have had the good fortune to do your city,
" but leave to return to my own country."
" Very well," fays he, " the Mocon will in a
" little time bring fhips for ivory. I will fend
" you home then, and give you wherewith to
" bear your charge." I thanked him again for
my liberty, and his good intentions toward me,
I ftaid with him expecting the Mocon ; and during that time, we made fo many journies to the
hill, that we filled our warehoufes with ivory, as
did the other merchants who traded in it.

The fhips arrived at laft, and my patron himfelf having made choice of the fhip wherein I
was to embark, he loaded half of it with ivory
on my account, he laid in provifions in abundance for my paffage, and befides obliged me to
accept a prefent of the curiofities of the country
of great value. After I had returned him a
thoufand thanks for all his favours, I went a-
board.

We ftopt at fome iflands to take in frefh provifions ; our veffel being come to a port on the
Terra Firma in the Indies, we touched there,
and not being willing to venture by fea to Balfora, I landed my proportion of the ivory, refolving to proceed on my journey by land. I made
vaft fums of my ivory. I bought feveral rarities
which I intended for prefents, and when my e-
quipage was got ready, I fet out in company of
a large caravan of merchants. I was a long
time on the way, and fuffered very much, but
endured all with patience, when I confidered
that I had nothing to fear from the feas, from
pirates, from ferpents, nor of the other perils I
had undergone.   ✦

All thefe fatigues ended at laft, and I came
fafe to Bagdad. I went immediately to wait
upon the Caliph, and gave him an account of
my embaffy. That prince told me, he had been
uneafy, by reafon I was fo long a returning, but
that he always hoped God would preferve me.
I told him the adventure of the elephants. He

reckoned this ſtory, and the other relations I had given him, to be ſo curious, that he ordered one of his ſecretaries to write them in characters of gold, and lay them up in his treaſury   I retired very well ſatisfied with the honours I received, and the preſents which he gave me ; and after that I gave myſelf up wholly to my family, kindred and friends.

FINIS.

www.ingramcontent.com/pod-product-compliance
Lightning Source LLC
Chambersburg PA
CBHW020804020726
47495CB00008B/2591